Pig Kahuna
Who's That PIG?

Jennifer Sattler

BLOOMSBURY
NEW YORK   LONDON   NEW DELHI   SYDNEY

First published in the United States of America in May 2015
by Bloomsbury Children's Books
www.bloomsbury.com

Bloomsbury is a registered trademark of Bloomsbury Publishing Plc

For information about permission to reproduce selections from this book, write to
Permissions, Bloomsbury Children's Books, 1385 Broadway, New York, New York 10018
Bloomsbury books may be purchased for business or promotional use. For information on bulk purchases
please contact Macmillan Corporate and Premium Sales Department at specialmarkets@macmillan.com

Library of Congress Cataloging-in-Publication Data
Sattler, Jennifer, author, illustrator.
Pig Kahuna : who's that pig? / by Jennifer Sattler.
pages   cm
ISBN 978-1-61963-632-3 (hardcover)
ISBN 978-1-61963-743-6 (e-book) • ISBN 978-1-61963-744-3 (e-PDF)
[1. Beaches—Fiction. 2. Brothers—Fiction. 3. Friendship—Fiction. 4. Pigs—Fiction.] I. Title.
PZ7.S24935Pk 2015   [E]—dc23   2014021978

Art created with acrylics and colored pencil
Typeset in Birdlegs
Book design by Nicole Gastonguay

Printed in China by Leo Paper Products, Heshan, Guangdong
2 4 6 8 10 9 7 5 3 1

All papers used by Bloomsbury Publishing, Inc., are natural, recyclable products
made from wood grown in well-managed forests. The manufacturing processes
conform to the environmental regulations of the country of origin.

For all the kids who are a little shy—
getting to know you is worth the wait!

To Fergus and Dink, it seemed like an ordinary Monday. A little collecting, a little building . . .

The beach was scattered
with the usual: rocks,
shells, seaweed.

But then they saw
something ... **someone**
who was anything **but** ordinary.

She could make sand angels.

She was fashionable.

And she was an excellent whistler.

"She can even stand on her head!"

"Let's go say hi!" said Dink. Fergus was nervous. He'd never seen anyone like this. "I don't know, maybe she wants to be alone."

"But she looks like so much fun!" insisted Dink.

Yoo-hoo!

Before Fergus could stop him, Dink was tottering right over to the strange pig.

"Hi!" said Dink.

"*Hola! Bonjour! Ciao!*" she answered. "I'm Tallulah."

Fergus watched from a
safe distance. Dink started
pointing. She was waving . . .
They were coming toward him!

Fergus tried to look busy.
"Tallulah, this is my big
brother, Fergus. He's a really
good digger!" Fergus blushed.

"Hi! You know, if you dig a deep-enough hole you can get to China! They use chopsticks there! 'Hi' in Chinese is '*nihao.*' It's fun to say . . ."

Fergus was speechless.

"Hey, Tallulah!
Wanna play with us?"
suggested Dink.

First, they played hide-and-seek. Fergus had always been good at hiding.

But Tallulah was even better.

Don't forget to breathe!

When it came to standing on her head, well, Tallulah was the best.

She even told really good jokes.

In fact, Tallulah and Dink were having so much fun they didn't seem to notice Fergus.

He was feeling a little left out.

But then something caught his eye.

Fergus had never seen a
crab this close. He didn't
really want to touch it.

"Have no fear, my little crabby friend!" shouted Tallulah. "Fergus will save you!"

"What should we do, Tallulah?" asked Dink. Tallulah sighed. "Well, when crabs are right side up, they are majestic creatures and excellent dancers!"

Fer-gus!

Fer-gus!

Fer-gus!

"Woo hoo!" shouted Tallulah.

"Three cheers for Fergus!"

"Let's all do the **crab!**"

"Oh, you're wonderful!
Magnifique! Fantastique!"
gushed Tallulah. "And Fergus . . ."

"Love the shirt!"